The Amazing Adventures of Abby McQuade

DAYLIGHT SAVING

Evan Jacobs

The Amazing Adventures of Abby McQuade

Back to the Past

Daylight Saving

The Ghosts of Largo Bay

The Lady from the Caves

Lucky Doll

Mazey Pines

The Morning People

Scream Night

TV Party

Virus

SADDLEBACK
EDUCATIONAL PUBLISHING
www.sdlback.com

ISBN: 978-1-68021-474-1
eBook: 978-1-63078-828-5

Printed in Malaysia

25 24 23 22 21   2 3 4 5 6

Largo Bay

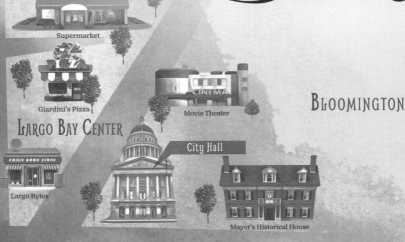

Supermarket

Giardini's Pizza

LARGO BAY CENTER

CINEMA

Movie Theater

BLOOMINGTON

City Hall

COMIC BOOK STORE

Largo Bytes

Mayor's Historical House

GATO VILLA

Adventure Begins

Time to Freak Out

A small earthquake sends the girls back in time. Are they now stuck in a time warp?

Fall Back

Abby and Clara are happy to get an extra hour
of sleep. Daylight Saving Time is finally over.

Wormhole

It's up to Abby to save the world.
Time will stop unless she can fix it.

CHAPTER 1

Fall Back

"Tikka is pretty amazing!" Abby McQuade said with a laugh. She was with Clara Erickson. The girls were best friends.

They watched an online video in Abby's bedroom. The room was simple. There was her large bed. The closet was full of clothes. She had a desk too. Like most kids, there was also a TV. It could stream shows. On the walls were photos of her friends.

Abby was on her bed. Clara lay on a blow-up mattress.

On the screen was a musician. She was called Tikka. The saxophone player was so good. She played pop music. When she played,

Tikka hung upside down. People loved her. The musician had over five million followers.

"How does she do it?" Clara asked. "How can she play like that?"

"Who cares? It's amazing!"

Clara was tan. Her hair was curly. Abby was fair. Her red hair stood out.

Abby loved to read. She was curious about everything. Archery was one of her hobbies. Her attitude was go with the flow.

Clara was a great swimmer. Every weekend she had swim meets. She wanted to compete in the Olympics. Her life was very scheduled.

"She can really play," Abby said. She was in awe over Tikka's skills.

"The songs don't sound boring," Clara said. "Even though she's just playing the sax."

It was just after two in the morning. Abby eyed her phone. "Sweet!" she said, laughing. "Daylight Saving Time is officially over."

Clara looked at her phone. "Saving?" she asked. "I thought it was *savings*."

"It's supposed to save daylight. That's why it is called saving. The idea started 100 years ago. It was during World War I," Abby said. "Then it was on again, off again. Congress made it consistent. This was in 1966. Spring forward and fall back, you know?"

"Wow. You're full of silly facts."

"Because I'm curious," Abby said, smirking.

Clara threw a pillow at her. "Why does the time change at two?" Clara asked. "Why not one?"

"Good question." Abby yawned. "I'll have to do some research. But guess what? We get an extra hour of sleep. It's so rad. Our phones will probably change soon."

"Ugh. I'm too tired to wait," Clara said. She yawned too. "Oh, here it is. My phone says it's one. Now let's get some sleep."

Both girls were suddenly tired. They kept watching Tikka. Eventually Abby and Clara nodded off.

-⋏⋏-

The ground seemed to move. Abby's one-story house shook slightly.

Abby woke up.

"Clara," she whispered. "Did you feel that? It was an earthquake."

"I thought it was a dream," Clara said. She sat up.

The girls looked at each other.

"Did anything fall?" Abby asked.

"Let's go look," Clara said.

"Okay."

The pair quickly walked out of Abby's bedroom.

A long hall ran the length of the house. All rooms could be entered through it. The front door opened into the living room. Then there were two options. One way was the kitchen. The other way was the hall. It led to the bedrooms. Abby's was first. Her parents' room was next. Another door in the hallway led to the garage.

Abby looked down the hall. Her parents' bedroom door was closed. "They probably slept through it," she said.

"It was small," Clara said.

The girls walked into the living room. It was fine. Bookshelves were bolted to the wall. The books hadn't fallen. None of the pictures had moved. The TV was still upright.

"What time is it?" Abby asked. She looked at her phone. 1:10 a.m. "Wait a minute."

"What?" Clara asked.

"It's only after one."

"Huh? We've only been asleep for 10 minutes."

"That's right." Abby held up her phone. "Why do I feel like I've slept all night?"

"I feel like I've slept too. Sometimes a nap

does that," Clara said. "It refreshes you. I take naps before swim meets."

"Uh-huh," Abby said. She plopped down onto the couch. "Time for more Tikka videos."

"Can we? Your parents won't be mad, will they?"

"We're not doing anything wrong." Abby smiled. "The earthquake woke us up."

Abby's parents were nice. She got along with them.

The TV clicked on. An old show was playing. Abby's dad liked watching oldies. He also enjoyed classic films.

The show was called *Diff'rent Strokes*. It was about two kids. Their mom had died. A rich man took them in. They made a new family. Everyone had fun together.

"Let's watch this," Clara said. "My dad likes this show too."

"No more Tikka?" Abby asked.

"Tikka is okay. Then she gets boring."

"Bite your tongue!"

The girls settled in. The 1980s clothes were funny. They especially loved watching the characters use a telephone. All they had were landlines!

The episode they watched was about Christmas. The characters' home had been burglarized. All the gifts had been stolen.

Finally the show ended. Another episode started up. Abby and Clara watched that one too.

"Are you sleepy?" Abby asked as the second episode ended.

"No," Clara said.

A third episode began. The theme song played.

"Do you want to watch?" Abby asked.

"Might as well." Clara shrugged.

The girls got ready for another show.

They would go back to Abby's room when they were sleepy.

Just then there was another small earthquake.

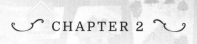

CHAPTER 2

Stuck in Time

Whoa!" Abby said. She looked at her bestie.

"Was that another quake?" Clara asked.

"It felt like one."

Abby looked around the living room. Nothing was out of place.

"Do you think your parents felt it?"

"I guess we'll know soon. They'll check on me."

The show's theme song played. Another episode was beginning.

"Didn't we just hear that song?" Clara asked.

"Maybe the quake affected the cable."

"But you have satellite TV," Clara said. "There are no earthquakes in space."

"Maybe it affected the wind. A strong wind could move the dish."

Clara snorted. "What are you talking about?"

"I don't know."

Both girls laughed. They cracked each other up.

The next show began. Minutes later they realized something. It was the Christmas episode again.

"Wait," Abby said. She sat up on the couch. "Didn't we already watch this?"

"Yeah. It started over."

"How?"

"I don't know," Clara said. "Maybe the earthquake reset the shows."

Abby eyed the TV box. Odd, the clock was wrong. It said 1:10 a.m.

"Clara? The clock went back."

"What?"

The girls looked at their phones. Both said 1:10 too.

"Weird. Why did it go back?" Abby asked.

"Has everything moved back? We should be in your room."

"This is sort of like *Groundhog Day*."

Abby had watched *Groundhog Day* with her parents. The movie was on TV every year. Usually it was around the holidays. One man lived the same day over and over. No matter what he did, the next day was the same.

"What if it doesn't end?" Clara asked. Her face dropped. She was a worrier.

Abby could see her friend getting stressed. "Let's go outside," she said. "Come on."

They should move around. Clara needed to be active. If not she would get anxious. This would make Abby nervous.

Abby took Clara's hand. She pulled her outside. The girls stood in the middle of their street. The Ericksons' house was across from the McQuades'. No lights were on.

Abby looked up and down the street. It was quiet outside.

"What are you looking for?" Clara asked.

"People."

"Why would anybody be out?"

"People are usually curious," Abby said. "Everyone goes outside after a quake. It's just like when we lose power. People get together. They check up on one another."

"It's really late."

"So?"

"They're probably asleep."

Abby looked at her. "You're right."

"I'm right? That's a first. About what?"

"Everybody *is* probably asleep. Things go unnoticed unless you're awake."

"Oh, right. Nobody would know that time is starting over."

"Well, not right away."

"What do you mean?" Clara asked.

"Our parents won't stay asleep forever."

Abby looked up at the sky. The stars looked different. Starlight moved slower. It left a trail.

"Look at the stars," she said.

Clara looked up.

"Do they look different to you?"

"Sort of," Clara said. "Let's go back inside. I don't want to get cold."

"Girl?" Abby pointed to Clara's clothes. "You're wearing a hoodie. It will be fine."

Both girls wore hoodies and pajama pants.

"Let's explore a little bit." Abby grinned. "Time doesn't change every night."

"Okay," Clara said. "But time usually doesn't get stuck either."

"Don't worry about it," Abby said. "Things will get unstuck."

"Let's just go back to bed. Why can't we be like everybody else?"

"Because we're not like everybody else."

"I know," Clara said. "That's the problem."

Abby grabbed Clara's arm. They moved to the sidewalk. "Even if we get caught—" Abby started.

"Let's not get caught," Clara snapped.

"Even if my parents wake up," Abby said. "It won't be bad."

"Oh yeah? How's that?" Clara asked.

"Well, time keeps going back, right? The latest we can really be out is now. It's just after one."

Clara glared at her friend. "Our curfew is nine o'clock!"

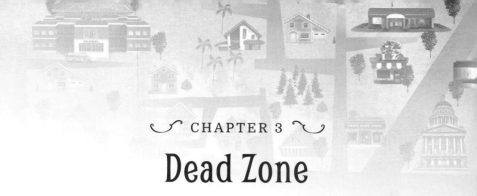

Dead Zone

Wow!" Abby said. "This town is really dead tonight."

"It always is," Clara said. "Look at the time!"

"Don't be silly. It's not that late. Some adults should be awake."

Clouds covered the moon. The sky was dark. Some streetlights weren't working.

The girls walked along Largo Bay Center. It was the largest strip mall in town. There were many shops. The best was Largo Bytes. The store sold video games and comic books. Abby and Clara liked to go there.

"Look at this place. The parking lot is empty. None of the lights are on." Abby pointed to the street. "No cars are on the road. This is weird. Is everyone asleep?"

"Maybe it's just a dead night. It happens, you know?"

Abby kept staring at the center.

The ground shook again.

The girls looked at each other. They checked their phones. 1:10 a.m.

"Well, here we are again. What do you want to do?" Abby asked.

"Go home."

"Clara!" Abby huffed. "That's no fun."

"Then why did you ask? I'm tired."

"Don't you find this interesting?" Abby put her arm around her bestie. "We're stuck in time. Something's going on."

"Maybe we need to go to sleep."

"Boring," Abby said with a laugh.

"No," Clara said. "I'm serious. Maybe that's it. We need to sleep it off."

"I doubt it," Abby said.

The girls walked for a bit. They didn't speak. Abby felt bad. Clara always tagged along on her adventures. Perhaps she really didn't like them.

"I'm sorry," Abby said.

"For what?"

"For making us come out here. I thought we might find something cool. Remember that time portal? This is a bust, though. I don't understand the earthquakes."

"Abby?" Clara put her arm around her friend. "I'm sorry. You know I like to complain. Your adventures are cool. I dig them."

"You do?"

"Most of the time."

The two laughed. They were different in many ways. Still, they could giggle about it.

"What are we going to do?" Clara asked. "The time is wrong."

"I have an idea," Abby said. "But it's weak. Let's tell my parents."

"Really?"

"Yes. This is weird. We can't stay in a time loop."

"Will they know what to do?"

"Maybe. My dad knows a lot about energy."

"Your mom does love math."

Abby's dad had his own business. It was called McQuade Solar. He loved his job. Solar energy was the future, he believed. It would save the environment. The world needed to be a better place for kids.

Abby's mom worked at a bank. She loved math. Her spare time was spent with math books. Spreadsheets were her jam. Abby couldn't believe it. Her mom did math problems for fun!

Would the adults figure out what was going on?

They headed toward Abby's house. Just then Abby heard a sound. It was faint. Then it got louder.

"Did you hear that?" Clara asked.

Abby turned around. A figure skated toward them. It was at the end of the street. In the darkness it looked scary.

"Who's that?" Abby asked.

"I don't know," Clara said. "Nobody we know. Who would be out?"

The figure skated closer.

"Hey!" the figure called out.

"Yikes!" Clara said. "Let's go."

Clara pulled on Abby's arm. They started to walk fast.

The skateboard clacked on the sidewalk. It didn't slow down.

"Hey!" the figure called again. "Abby! Clara!"

"Who is it?" Abby whispered.

"Who cares?" Clara said.

Clara started to run. She pulled Abby along with her.

The girls turned a corner. Now they were in their neighborhood. The streetlights were bright.

Abby and Clara ran through the streets.

The board's wheels were clacking. The stranger was closing in on them.

"Cut through the park!" Abby said.

"Wait. Why?"

"There's too much grass for the board. Then we can hop the brick wall."

"You can't hop that wall," Clara said. "It's too high."

True. Abby didn't like the wall. Kids jumped it all the time. The wall was too high for her. She didn't like heights.

"Come on!" Abby cried.

She grabbed Clara now. They ran into the park.

There was a playground. It was popular with families. The girls liked to hang out there.

There was a street on the other side of the wall. The street was close to home.

The pair sprinted across the grass. One sidewalk went through the park. But it didn't go near the wall.

The boarder stopped skating. Now the figure was on foot.

The girls ran to the brick wall. Clara tried to climb it. She couldn't get a good grip. Her fingers slipped off.

Abby tried to climb too. Her fingers couldn't reach the top.

The two turned. There had to be another way. But it was too late. The stranger was there.

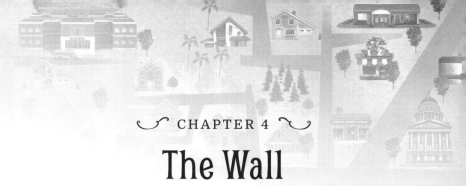

CHAPTER 4

The Wall

Why were you running?" It was Tim Cadena. "Didn't you hear me calling?"

Tim wore pajamas. He had on a long flannel robe. Without the light, it had looked like a cape.

"You creeper!" Abby snapped. "Were you trying to scare us?"

"No! I wasn't. I swear!" Tim said. "Didn't you know it was me? I called your names."

"How should we know?" Clara asked.

"Duh, by my voice." Tim rolled his eyes.

"You were acting creepy," Abby said. "Next time say your name. It's late. You could have been anyone."

"Fine!" Tim ran a hand through his hair. "I'm sorry for scaring you."

"Who says you scared us?" Abby asked.

Abby and Tim always argued. Clara said it was because they liked each other. Abby denied it. How did Tim really feel? She was curious.

"You said it," Tim said, grinning. "Why were you running? Only scaredy-cats run."

"Why are you out so late anyway?" Clara asked.

"Why are *you* out so late?" Tim clapped back. "I snuck out. It was hard to sleep. Skating relaxes me. My parents would kill me if they knew. Then the earthquake hit. Did you feel it? I almost ate the sidewalk. That's when I noticed the time change. It didn't fall back. I was stoked," he said. "Then there was another quake. That's when I found you two."

"Why didn't you tell your parents?" Abby asked.

"Did you tell yours?" Tim said.

Abby and Clara didn't reply.

"That's what I thought," he said. "You two are dorks. The way you tried to hop the wall. It was hilarious!"

"Like you could do it?" Abby said.

"Watch this." He threw his skateboard over the wall. It landed with a thump on the other side.

"I hope it broke!" Abby hissed.

"Me too!" Clara said.

Tim stepped back. Then he ran to the wall. He climbed it easily.

"Wow," he teased, sitting on the wall. "That was *so* hard."

"Humph!" Clara said. She stepped back too. Why couldn't an athlete scale the wall? Her fingers caught the top as she made a perfect jump. Clara pulled herself up.

"Not bad," Tim said. He clapped a few times. "Abby won't be able to do it."

"She can totally do it!"

The pair stared down at Abby.

Abby stepped back. She wasn't athletic. Could she do it?

"Come on, girl!" Clara cheered.

"Boo!" Tim smirked.

Abby took a deep breath. Then she ran toward the wall. Her fingers hit the brick. The wall felt brittle under her hands. Abby kicked her legs. Using all her might, she pulled herself upward. No way could she fail. Tim would mock her for eternity.

"Aahhh!" Abby cried. Then she pulled herself to the top. Yes! She'd done it. Only she couldn't look down. It would make her dizzy.

"Way to go!" Clara smiled.

The girls high-fived.

"Good job," Tim said.

He hopped down with ease. Clara did the

same. Abby just sat there. She looked at her best friend.

"Do you need help?" Clara asked.

Before Abby could answer, her phone rang.

CHAPTER 5

Call for Help

Abby looked at her classmates. Her phone kept ringing. The screen didn't call out the number.

"Who is it?" Clara asked.

"Unavailable."

"Whoa," Tim said, laughing. "Abby gets unlisted calls after one."

"Shut up!" Abby answered the call. "Hello?" she said.

"There's something wrong with the time. Did you notice?" Abby recognized the voice immediately.

"Grandma McQuade!" Abby smiled.

Mrs. McQuade was in her mid-70s. The lady was a straight shooter. She could be feisty too. In the 1960s she was a government agent. Her job was top secret. Nobody knew what it was. Grandma McQuade's lips were sealed.

"How are you?" Abby asked.

"Well, I've been better. Time needs to stop falling back to one o'clock!" Grandma McQuade said. "It's driving me bonkers. Those quakes are real shakers."

"What's going on?" Abby asked. "Do you know? My parents are sleeping. So are Clara's. We've been trying to figure it out."

"I'll tell you in person," Grandma said. "Someone might be listening in. I don't trust these phones. Let me just say this. It's going to get worse. A lot worse. When can you two be here?"

"What? You mean now?" Abby eyed Clara and Tim.

Tim seemed confused. He didn't know anything about Abby's grandma.

Clara shook her head no.

"It makes the most sense," her grandma said. "Don't you think? I don't drive at night. Accidents happen in the dark. Then we'd be in a pickle. I called Amtrak Eddie too. He might not be fast enough. This time thing needs to stop. Everything's going to fall back!"

Amtrak Eddie was Abby's favorite uncle. He loved to hear about her adventures. His advice was the best.

Eddie was a train engineer for Amtrak. He had been one for 20 years. The world was full of crazy stories. Abby's uncle had seen it all.

"What do you mean by that? What's going to fall back?" Abby asked.

The ground shook again.

Abby grabbed on to the wall. This earthquake was stronger than the others. She almost fell. "Hello?" she said into the phone. "Grandma? Are you still there?"

"Yes," her grandma said.

Something was off. Her own voice sounded different. Why? She couldn't put her finger on it.

"Abby," Clara called. She held up her phone. "That shaker didn't stick to the schedule."

"Right. It felt stronger."

"No," Clara said. "That's not it. The quakes were coming every hour. Every time the clock hit one. The last one hit after 45 minutes."

"Grandma," Abby said into the phone. "The earthquake happened sooner. Clara has been timing them."

"I know," Grandma McQuade said. "I'm timing them too. We need to hurry. My mini-seismograph is all set up."

Grandma McQuade's voice sounded dull. It had lost some of its feistiness. She spoke without energy.

There had to be a connection. Maybe the earthquakes were damaging the phone lines.

"Things are falling back," her grandma said. "The earthquakes will be more frequent. Time will stop moving at all. It will freeze. So will we! Everyone on Earth will be stuck."

"Is that why your voice sounds different?" Abby asked. "It's getting slower."

"Yes, it's happening," Grandma McQuade said. "Enough of this lollygagging. We've got the world to save!"

"Oh my gosh," Abby said. "We'll be right over. Can I ask one question?"

"Fire away," her grandma said.

"Should I tell my parents?" Abby asked. "This affects them too. Maybe they can help us."

"Normally I'd say yes. Time is the problem here. We can't stop the mission. Too much time will be lost. Convincing them will take forever. Sadly, we can't afford it!"

CHAPTER 6

A Space Event

The sky looks amazing!" Abby said.

The stars and moon were bright. Both left light trails. Somehow the light moved slower. Why was it happening?

Before, the stars had short trails. Now the paths of light looked longer. It made the night sky brighter.

The three kids walked down the street. They were trying to move quickly. But they couldn't.

"Wow, it's hard to move," Tim said.

"I'm slow," said Clara.

"Cool but weird," Abby said. "It's like we're walking through Jell-O."

Grandma McQuade didn't live too far from Abby. Her condo was in Largo Woods. It was for seniors only.

"I just saw a shooting star!" Clara said.

Abby almost never noticed shooting stars. Tonight was different. The falling stars were everywhere. They left long white trails. Everyone knew the "stars" were really space rocks.

"Okay," Tim said. "Why do you guys sound funny? Stop it."

"We can't stop," Abby said. "I told you what my grandma said. Things are slowing down."

"That doesn't explain it," he snapped. Tim dropped his skateboard to the ground. He got on and skated.

"She said time is falling back," Abby said. "Take action or it will continue."

"Could we be frozen in time?" Clara asked.

"Maybe."

"May-be," Tim teased. He lowered his tone.

"Why are you joking?" Abby asked. "Your voice sounds weird too."

"It doesn't to me," Tim said. He did an ollie on his board. "Whoa! That was epic."

-ᴘᴧ-

The kids finally reached Grandma McQuade's condo. They sat in the living room. The room had a huge bookcase but no TV.

"Grandma?" Abby asked. "What is all this stuff?"

Grandma McQuade had set up a table. It was in the middle of the room. On the table was a small green screen. Every few seconds a beam of light circled on the screen. In the center was a dot. It was supposed to be Earth.

Next to the screen was a small machine. It was a seismograph. The machine tracked movement. There was a little black box next to it. A large red button was on top. The box was the size of a Rubik's Cube.

"I went undercover at NASA. These are my goodies."

"You worked at NASA?" Clara asked.

"Sure did," Grandma McQuade said. "But don't ask questions. My lips are sealed. Can't tell you even if I wanted to."

"What's NASA?" Tim asked.

Everyone gasped.

"National Aeronautics and Space Administration. Duh!" Abby snapped. "Who doesn't know that?" She didn't mean to sound harsh. They needed to fix what was happening.

"No insults. Good vibes only," Abby's grandma said. "We need to work together."

"I'm sorry," Abby said to Tim.

"It's okay," he said. "I was just punking you."

"NASA keeps its eye on space," Grandma McQuade said. "It knows what's going on up there. This machine is legit. It works well. Now I know what's happening above and below."

"And?" Clara asked. "What *is* happening?"

"Hmm, okay ..." Grandma McQuade took a deep breath. "I'll spill. You can never repeat this. *Ever.* The world can't handle it."

The three teens promised.

"This event happens every 50 years," Abby's grandma said. "Fifty years ago, I had just started my job. But I can't tell you what it was."

"Top-secret spy stuff?" Tim said. "How cool!"

"Yeah. It *was* cool. Every 50 years, a comet and an asteroid collide. These two rocks are each about the size of Earth. The crash happens in the fall. It sends shockwaves around the galaxy. Protons get trapped in the wave. This interrupts everything. Planets stop spinning. Earth spins on its axis. You get how that works, right?"

"Yeah," the kids said. They were staring at Grandma McQuade. Their eyes were wide.

It took a day for Earth to do one rotation. The planet also revolved around the sun. This took an entire year.

"The shockwaves have slowed us down. We are moving slower. Did you notice?"

They all nodded.

"It took us forever to get here," Abby said.

"Our voices sound funny too," Clara said.

"Have you seen the sky, Mrs. McQuade?" Tim asked.

"You bet I have," Grandma McQuade said. "Things will only get slower."

Suddenly the ground shook. It was another earthquake. It felt stronger than the last one.

Abby was scared. Her grandma knew what

she was talking about. Things were going to get worse. They had to do something.

Grandma McQuade checked the machine. "Those quakes are 40 minutes apart," she said. "Soon they'll stop."

"What happens then?" Tim asked.

"We'll stop," Abby said.

Tim, Abby, and Clara stared at Grandma McQuade.

"Abby's correct," she said. "We will stop moving. If that happens, Earth will lose its orbit. The planet won't spin. Life as we know it will be frozen in time. We'll float for eternity."

"So this happens every 50 years?" Abby asked.

"Yes. And it has always been fixed. I was much younger the last time. Now I'm an old lady."

The teens laughed nervously.

"That's why I need you," Grandma McQuade said. "People have never failed before. It will be okay! Time to get to work."

CHAPTER 7

The Plan

"Let me drive!" Tim said.

Abby was sitting in the driver's seat. Everyone was in Grandma McQuade's car. She was riding shotgun. In her hand was the small black box with the red button. Clara and Tim sat in the back.

Grandma McQuade's car was always messy. Sometimes there was food she'd forgotten about. Junk mail piled up on the floor. Abby joked that it was a mobile trash can.

"We can't let you drive," Abby said. "You'd probably crash."

"I drive my brother's car sometimes," Tim said. "I've never crashed."

"You're a liar," Clara snapped.

"No I'm not. I've got skills."

"It doesn't really matter," Abby's grandma said. "We can't speed anyway."

"Oh, right," Abby said. The gas pedal was pressed to the floor. Everything had slowed down. Everyone talked slower. Nobody moved quickly. That included machines.

The car went 20 miles per hour. It would not go faster.

"Look on the bright side," Grandma McQuade said. "Nobody is getting a speeding ticket!" She laughed hard at her own joke.

"Man, I wish I could skate right now," Tim said. "My tricks would be epic!"

Abby eyed the sky. The stars were bright. Moonlight flooded the planet. "Look at the sky," she said. "It's like the universe has slowed down."

"It has," Grandma McQuade said. "This is a first. I've never seen anything like it."

"You haven't?" the kids asked at once.

Grandma McQuade had seen it all. If something surprised her, things must be bad.

"Um ... what is our plan?" Abby asked.

"This!" Grandma McQuade said. She held up the black box. "This is a sound machine. Hit this red button." She pointed to the top of the box. "What's the tallest point in town?" she asked.

"Largo Hills," Abby said. "Right above the wetlands."

"We need to go there," her grandma said. "This sound box needs to get shot into the sky. Hit this button. Three seconds later it will explode. *Boom!* It is a sound-wave bomb. The sound travels super fast. Humans can't hear it," she said. "The waves are powerful. This should get the planet back on track. Everything will return to normal."

"Really?" Abby asked. "What are our chances?"

"It is a long shot," her grandma said.

"Ugh," Clara said. "The wetlands are on the other side of town. We're not even close. I'm not sure we'll make it."

"How are we going to launch that box?" Tim frowned. "We'll need a huge slingshot, right?"

"My archery set!" Abby said excitedly. "Why didn't you ask me to bring it?"

"Hold your horses," Grandma McQuade said. "It's after one o'clock. I'm of a certain age. There's a heavy weight on my shoulders. Nobody's perfect! Turn right here. Your house is around the corner."

The car pulled up in front of Abby's house.

"Hurry!" Grandma McQuade said.

Everyone's voice had slowed again. Just then there was another earthquake. The last one had been 30 minutes ago. The ground shook with force.

"Okay," Abby replied. "I ... will ... hurry." Her voice sounded weird.

Abby stepped toward the front door. Her legs felt heavy. Moving an inch seemed impossible. She forced her brain to control her feet. Every step was slow. It took five minutes to reach the door.

"Qu-ick-er!" Clara called. It sounded like she was underwater. Her voice slowly cut through the air.

Abby ignored her bestie. She had to stay focused. It took a minute to get her key. Putting it into the lock was tough. Finally the lock clicked.

She was inside!

The living room was dark. It was hard to see. Abby walked slowly through the room.

A few minutes passed.

She was almost to the hallway.

This isn't going to work, she thought.

How will I launch that box? I can hardly move. There is no point in worrying now. First things first. Get the archery set. Worry later.

Her parents' bedroom door opened. Abby's mom slowly stepped out.

CHAPTER 8

Time Repeats

Ab-by!" her mom said dully. "What ... are ... you ... doing?" she asked.

"Mom!"

Whoa. Abby couldn't believe it. It was almost funny. They sounded ridiculous. But the situation was critical. Time was almost up.

"There's no time to explain. I need my archery set."

Abby moved past her mom. It was awkward. She walked sluggishly. Would her mother stop her?

It took five more minutes to reach her bedroom.

"Ab-by!" her mom said.

She was coming after her!

Abby turned on her bedroom light. The archery set was across the room. It was leaning against her desk.

"Darn it!" she said.

"What?" her mom asked. "Why are you acting like this?"

The set was 10 feet away. Yet it was too far.

Abby moved across her room. It didn't seem real. She knew every corner. Now she walked through it like she was trapped in quicksand.

Each step was painfully slow. Abby never took her eyes off the goal. She had to get the bow and arrows.

Mrs. McQuade kept asking her to stop. Abby was getting tired. The effort took so much energy. Finally she reached her bow.

Now her mom blocked the exit. "What are you up to?" she asked. "We need to talk. Right now, young lady."

Abby thought about jumping through the window. No. It would take too long. Her mom would stop her.

"Mom!" Abby yelled. "Please trust me."

Mrs. McQuade looked shocked. Her daughter had never yelled at her before.

Maybe her mom would understand. Abby had to try to explain. But time was running out. Another earthquake hit suddenly.

Abby fell onto the bed. She looked up at the ceiling. *Is it over?* she wondered. *What a crazy dream.*

"Clara?" she called out. Abby looked at her friend. No, this wasn't a dream. Time was still falling back.

Clara stared at her. "How come I'm here?" she asked. "What just happened?"

Their voices were low and lazy. It was almost time to freak out.

"I don't know!" Abby said. She sat up slowly.

"Where's Tim?"

Abby grabbed her phone.

"What are you doing?" Clara asked.

"Texting Tim," Abby said. "I want to make sure he's okay."

"U kewl?" she wrote. It took a few minutes to tap.

"What did he say?" Clara asked.

Abby's phone was blank. Then it dinged.

"Kewl. Home. Slow. Can't move."

"10-4," Abby wrote back. "Stay safe."

Nothing was going as planned. Everything took too long. Abby realized how much she'd taken for granted.

"Time is going too slow," Abby said. "We're back where we started."

"No," Clara whined. "We're going to fail! Time will stop!"

"We've got to try!" She slowly stood up.

Abby's adventures were usually all action.

It wasn't possible now. She grabbed the bow and arrows.

Clara moved to the door.

"Let's do this!" Abby yelled. She didn't care who heard her. They had to make it happen. Otherwise all would be lost.

It was time to save the world!

The girls made it outside. They moved as quickly as possible. Abby held on to her archery set.

The sky was bright. It looked like morning.

"Abby!" Clara warned. "Another shaker is coming."

"We … more … need … time," Abby said. Her words were mixed up.

Clara looked scared.

A pickup truck appeared out of nowhere. It was moving fast. How was it possible?

It screeched to a stop. The door opened.

CHAPTER 9

Wormholes

Grandma McQuade! "Get in!" she shouted. For a second her voice sounded normal.

Abby's grandma was in the passenger seat. Amtrak Eddie was driving. The sound box was in Grandma McQuade's lap.

"Come on, girls," Amtrak Eddie said. His voice sounded normal too.

Was everything okay?

The girls climbed into the truck. Abby put her archery set between them. They moved quickly. It felt great.

"All right," Grandma McQuade said. "Hit it, Eddie!"

Suddenly her grandma's voice slowed again.

Eddie hit the gas. The truck inched forward.

"What happened?" Abby asked. It took her forever to speak. "Everything seemed okay."

"How did you guys get here so fast?" Clara asked.

"Don't you remember?" Grandma McQuade said. Her voice practically crawled. "I called him right away. Now time is resetting. That's why you ended up back home. Thank goodness our memories don't reset."

It took Grandma McQuade five minutes to say that. As she talked, she typed. Directions to Largo Hills popped up.

"Will we ever get there?" Abby asked. Her voice was unrecognizable. "We're too far away. The truck is barely moving."

"Just wait," Amtrak Eddie said. "Wormholes let us travel fast. Especially when they collapse. That's how we'll beat this. It's how we got here."

"Wormholes?" Clara asked.

"Shortcuts through the universe," Abby said. "Aren't those in space?"

"Oh yeah," Amtrak Eddie said. "They *are* in space but also on Earth. Space and time are pokey now. This trip is like moving through the universe. I make my living on a train. Knowing about wormholes is good business sense. I do it every day."

Abby and Clara rolled their eyes. What was Amtrak Eddie talking about? Could they beat this or not?

"How do you find these wormholes?" Abby asked.

Abby's uncle snorted. "They're everywhere. People never think about it. You just need to open your eyes."

Then he pointed to his phone. It showed an image of the truck. The truck moved on a map. Obviously it was a GPS location.

"Look closer. This isn't ordinary GPS. I can find wormholes with this. It's not on the market yet. My friend in India coded it for me."

Abby and Clara eyed Grandma McQuade.

"What are you looking at me for?" she said. "He's always been into this stuff."

"See?" Eddie said. "We're going to win. Everything will be okay."

He pointed to the phone again. On the screen a tree icon blinked. Amtrak Eddie turned the wheel hard.

"It doesn't feel like we're moving," Abby said.

"If this wormhole fails, we won't be!" Grandma McQuade warned.

"Wait a minute!" Clara said. She pointed out the window. "We're going to hit that tree!"

An enormous tree was directly ahead. Its trunk was huge. There were hundreds of branches. Behind it was a two-story house.

"Hold the phone!" Abby said. "Are we going to crash into that tree? Is that why your phone is blinking? Is it a wormhole?"

"So many questions! Just wait. We want to get to Largo Hills," Eddie said. He gripped the steering wheel. "The sound machine has to work. This is the quickest way. Wormholes are all around us. What's in Largo Hills? Trees! This tree is a wormhole."

"This is crazy," Clara said.

"It had better work," Abby said. "Or we'll be toast."

The truck inched toward the tree. It was slow going. Would it work? They weren't moving fast enough.

"Uncle Eddie!" Abby said. She was frustrated. "I don't know about this. Everything needs to go back like it was. Time has to be normal again."

The girls held their breath. The truck slowly moved into the tree. It didn't crash!

Everything disappeared.

Abby couldn't feel her body. She couldn't see anything. Was she dead?

CHAPTER 10

Set Your Clocks

Zoom! Bam! Crack! The truck was surrounded by light. Then Abby saw trees.

"Taht saw looc!" Abby said. Her voice was still slow. The words were a garbled mess.

The truck barely moved.

"I think we did it!" Amtrak Eddie called. He looked around.

Largo Hills was dark. There were no streetlights. The moon and stars were shining. That helped.

"Wait a minute," Grandma McQuade said nervously. She *never* freaked out. Uh-oh.

Now Abby was starting to worry.

"We're at the bottom of the hill!" Abby's grandma said.

"That we are," Amtrak Eddie said.

He stepped on the gas. It didn't help. The engine revved. That was about it. The truck put-putted up the hill. It was like a golf cart.

"No! We will never make it," Clara whined.

"Snap out of it," Amtrak Eddie said. "Stay positive!" He kept his eyes on the road. "Time is relative, right? So are wormholes. This one got us close."

Eddie chuckled. It didn't sound like a nervous laugh. He never seemed to worry about anything.

Just then the truck began to shake.

Abby looked around. Wait! What? The back of the truck was gone! It was still in the darkness of the wormhole.

"Eddie?" Abby said. She tried to speak clearly. "Why is half the truck missing?"

"It is?" her uncle asked. He looked into the rearview mirror. "Well, what do you know?"

"Huh? About what?" Clara asked. "What's happening?"

The truck continued up the hill. They were not going to make it. Largo Bay's highest point was unreachable. Time would reset. All would be lost.

Next time they would be lucky if they remembered. Abby was scared. She hid her fear from Clara.

"We must still be in the wormhole," Eddie said.

"What?" the girls said.

"Well, then step on it!" Grandma McQuade ordered.

"It's starting to collapse," he said.

The truck shook again. This time it felt like it would fall apart.

"Uncle Eddie, this feels wrong," Abby said. "What does it mean?"

"I have an idea," he said. "You know how water drips from a faucet?"

"What does dripping water have to do with it?" Grandma McQuade barked. "We're trying to keep time moving here. The world needs saving."

"With a slow drip, the water pinches off. Then it drips away," he said. "A wormhole does the same thing. It should give us some momentum. If we're lucky."

"The wormhole is collapsing," Abby said. She was a good student. But this science talk wasn't easy for her to grasp. "Will it crush us?"

"I guess it could," he said. "But I doubt it. The front of the truck is in real time. The back of the truck is stuck. Maybe it will get crushed. I don't know. It's all a theory. Nobody's ever experienced this before."

Suddenly the truck moved forward. Eddie's foot was still on the gas. It tore up the hill. The truck moved like a rocket.

Whoosh!

"Sweet!" Eddie screamed. "I guess we pinched off from the wormhole. The back end is still here too. It didn't crush it or us!"

The truck continued to zoom upward.

"Here!" Grandma McQuade said. She handed the sound box to Abby. A piece of string was wrapped around the red button. "We're almost to the top. It's the highest point in town. You give that red button a whack. Then shoot it into the air with your bow and arrow."

"Okay," Abby said. This was crazy. Would it work? Her grandma said it would. Abby had faith.

Everyone's voice had returned to normal. It lasted for a second. Then their voices sped up. The sounds were high and squeaky. Abby was used to the slow talking. The pace now was insane.

The truck continued upward. It was 10 yards from the highest hill. Suddenly the truck slowed down. It went slower than ever. Abby and Clara looked at each other. Was it rolling backward?

"No!" Abby cried.

"This can't happen," Clara wept.

Abby grabbed her bow and arrow. She held the sound box tightly.

Clara knew what her bestie was about to do. She opened the door to the truck.

Abby jumped out. Then she took off running.

"Good luck!" Clara screamed.

Somehow Abby was superhuman. She ran faster than she had ever run. Was this speed from the wormhole? Now wasn't the time to ask questions.

Thump! Thump! Thump! Her heart pounded hard in her chest.

Abby was almost to the peak. She could see the wetlands below. The wide ocean was beyond it. There were no waves. The wind was nonexistent. It was a weird feeling. This was the breeziest part of the city.

The sky had turned white. Ribbons of light from the moon and stars lit up the heavens. It would have been beautiful. But this meant the end of time.

Suddenly Abby felt something. Her feet were impossibly heavy. She could barely lift them. The bow and arrow weighed a ton. So did the little sound box.

Abby shook it off. She had to keep moving. Stopping now meant stopping forever.

Trees and patches of grass were on both sides of her. Abby had reached the peak. The next half mile was downhill. It led into the wetlands.

Her legs felt like they were stuck in cement. For sure she would stop moving at any moment. Suddenly the ground shook.

It was another earthquake. This one felt massive.

Oh no! she thought. *This is it! What if I wake up in my room? Time will be over. Earth is finished.*

"Aahhh!" she screamed out loud.

With everything she had, Abby leaped into the air. Her movements were in slow motion. It felt like she was flying. She tapped the red button.

In the next second, she attached the box to her arrow. She placed the arrow into her bow. It was a graceful movement. Her right arm and elbow thrust back.

Ping! She let go. The arrow soared into the sky.

In the pickup everyone gasped.

"Whee!" Abby yelled. She could do no more. Every ounce of energy was gone.

Kaboom! Kaboom!

The sound box exploded. Waves of sound moved through the air. They rippled against the light. It was a tidal wave of sound.

Streaks of light reversed course. A thousand protons exploded at once. In an instant, the night had returned. It was normal once more.

The sky looked almost black. Stars twinkled. The moon glowed.

Abby crashed to the ground. She rolled as she fell. A rock hit her in the ribs. It hurt but not too much.

Two lights came toward her. She could hear the roar of an engine. Doors slammed. Then everything turned black.

"Wait. She's okay." It was Uncle Eddie.

"Her pupils are reacting," Grandma McQuade said.

"Abby?" Clara said.

"It worked!" Abby said with joy. Her eyes

popped open. "Did you see? Best jump ever!"

"Oh, honey," Grandma McQuade said. "You did it. I knew you would. Way to go!"

"This time I can't blame you," Clara said. "But ..." her voice trailed off.

"But what?" Abby asked.

"Why you? Why us? There are billions of people," Clara said. She looked confused.

"Great skills," Grandma McQuade declared. "Adventure finds the heroes. It always has. Good going, kids. The Earth will keep spinning. This time it was a little too close. We could have been cooked."

"I couldn't have done it without my wingman," Abby said. She hugged Clara tightly.

Uncle Eddie squeezed her shoulder. Grandma McQuade checked her for broken bones.

Abby put her bow into the truck. "We all

helped," she said. "It feels good to see the moon like this."

The four of them took a walk. They looked at the ocean. It disappeared into the horizon.

"Everything seems fine," Eddie said. He took out some binoculars. "The stars are shining as they should."

Clara launched an app. It showed where the stars were. "Look," Clara said. "The Big Dipper. There's Orion's Belt." She pointed upward.

"Hey, that's a cool app," Grandma McQuade said.

"You can't use it on a flip phone," Abby said.

"Humph!" said her grandma.

"Wait," Clara said. "It's just after one again. Time will fall back at two. Am I right? It falls back an hour."

"It should," Abby said. "Right, Grandma?"

"Correct," Grandma McQuade said. "Don't forget to set your clocks."

"Most digital clocks do it for you," Amtrak Eddie said. "Oh, back in the day I had to change a lot of clocks."

"What should we do?" Abby asked. "I can't sleep now." She was thrilled everything had worked out. No more weird voices. Hopefully the earthquakes were over.

"Do?" Grandma McQuade asked. "Let's get into this truck. I'm tired. It's time to sleep."

Clara yawned. "Me too," she said. She walked over to the pickup.

Abby looked at her uncle.

"How do you like that?" He grinned. "We just saved the world. All anyone wants to do is sleep."

"Do you know what's cool? Falling back is cool!" Abby said. "We get to sleep an extra hour. I'm going to need it."

Everyone climbed into the truck. Amtrak Eddie started the engine. Then he turned the wheel and headed back.

Abby rolled down the window. A gentle ocean breeze blew. Fresh air filled the truck. In two seconds the girls were asleep.

Eddie and Grandma McQuade chuckled silently. "Kids these days," they whispered.

The Amazing Adventures of
Abby McQuade

More Amazing Adventures with Abby

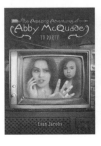